THIS WALKER BOOK BELONGS TO:

_____

_____

_____

_____

*For my
darling Amy*
A.D.

*For
Julie Chalmers*
S.H.

First published 1995 by
Walker Books Ltd
87 Vauxhall Walk
London SE11 5HJ

This edition published 1996

10 9 8 7 6 5 4 3 2 1

Text © 1995 Alan Durant
Illustrations © 1995 Sue Heap

This book has been typeset
in Providence Sans and Roman.

Printed in Hong Kong

British Library Cataloguing
in Publication Data
A catalogue record for
this book is available
from the British Library.

ISBN 0-7445-4390-8

Alan Durant

MOUSE PARTY

illustrated by
Sue Heap

WALKER BOOKS
AND SUBSIDIARIES
LONDON • BOSTON • SYDNEY

Mouse found a deserted house and decided to make his home there. But it was a very big house for such a small mouse and he felt a little lonely. "I know," he thought, "I'll have a party." So he sent invitations to all his friends.

The first
to arrive were

Cat with a **mat** and

Dog with a **log**.

Then came **Hare** with a **chair,**

Owl with a **towel**,

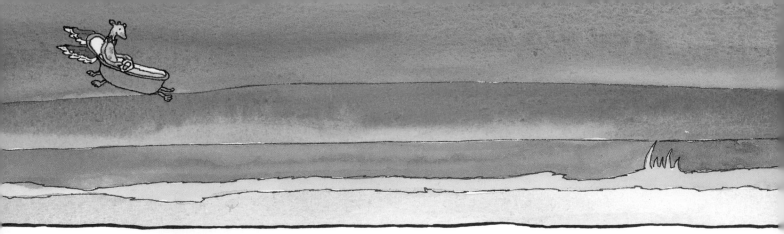

Giraffe with a **bath,**

Hen with a **pen**,

Lamb with some jam,

Rat with a **bat** in a **hat,**

and **Fox** with a **box** full of **lots**

and colours of **socks**.

and **lots** of different kinds

"Let's party!" said Mouse.   But...

Rat- a-

tat - tat!

It was an elephant with two trunks.
He was blowing through one and
carrying the other.
"Hello," said Mouse. "Welcome to my house."

"Your house?" said the elephant
and he looked rather cross.
"I've just been away on a long holiday.
This house, I must tell you, is mine!"

"Oh," said Mouse, Lamb, Hare, Rat, and Bat.

"Oh," said Hen, Dog, Owl, Fox, and Giraffe.

But, "Come in, come in!" said Cat.
"You're just in time for the party."

"A party . . . for me?" said Elephant.
"Oh my! Yippee!"

So they drank and they ate and they danced

until late and had the most marvellous party.

And later, when the guests had
all gone home, leaving Elephant
and Mouse alone, Elephant said,
"I think, little Mouse, perhaps
it's true, there's room for us
both in this house, don't you?"

MORE WALKER PAPERBACKS
For You to Enjoy

TOWN PARROT
by Penelope Bennett/Sue Heap

The story of Turkey, a Blue-fronted Amazon parrot,
and the person she lives with, Ann. It's full of fascinating facts about parrots.

"A small masterpiece, superbly crafted… Quite superb
and a must for all primary classrooms." *The School Librarian*

0-7445-4727-X   £4.99

MY CAT JACK
by Pat Casey

"This beautiful book is simply a celebration of the animal yawning,
stretching, scratching, purring and washing,
with some of the best drawings of a cat I have ever seen."
Anthony Browne, The Financial Times

0-7445-4360-6   £4.50

IT'S MY BIRTHDAY
by Helen Oxenbury

A toddler enlists the help of some animal friends
to find the ingredients for a birthday cake.

"Small children will love the sense of repetition in this story,
leading to the happy ending when all the friends sit
down together to demolish the cake." *Parents*

0-7445-4344-4   £3.99